THE USBORNE BOOK

PUPPETS

Ken Haines and Gill Harvey

Ken Haines is a professional puppeteer with extensive TV, stage and workshop experience.

Designed by Ian McNee • Illustrated by Teri Gower
Photographs by Howard Allman and Ray Moller
Editor: Felicity Brooks • Managing designer: Mary Cartwright
Puppets made by Rachel Wells

With thanks to Red Madrell, Tanya Noble, Claire Hurley and Jahneen Cousins

Contents

About making puppets

Getting ready

This book shows you how to make many kinds of puppets, from sock puppets to string puppets. Ones nearer to the back of the book are a little more difficult to make, but well worth the effort. Before you start, it's a good idea to read through these two pages. There are some useful hints about the different techniques and materials you will use.

If you are going to use a craft knife, pliers or a skewer, ask an adult to help you.

Read through the instructions and make sure you have everything you need.

Put on an apron, as glue doesn't always wash out of clothes.

What you will need

You may find some materials around the house – empty plastic bottles, newspaper, cardboard, kitchen foil and so on. Others, such as fabric, felt, yarn, wire and wooden sticks, are fairly cheap and can be found in department stores, craft or hardware stores.

You probably have the basic equipment that you need – a pencil, scissors, a ruler and glue, so the instructions don't always mention them (but see the note on page 3 about glue). Sometimes you need other things such as a craft knife, pliers or a skewer, so you may need to buy or borrow them.

Cover your work surface with newspaper to protect it from glue.

Templates

Templates are the shapes you use as guides for cutting things out. At the back of the book, there are some outlines for you to copy and make into templates. You need thin cardboard, tracing paper, a soft pencil and scissors.

1. Place tracing paper over the outline. Draw over it firmly with a soft pencil.

2. Turn the tracing paper over. Place it on cardboard. Scribble firmly over all the lines.

3. Draw over the lines again to make them clearer, then cut the shape out.

Rectangles and circles

For rectangles and circles, the book just gives measurements. You can make the templates using a ruler for straight edges and a compass for circles. If you don't have a compass, you could use a plate or lid of about the right size.

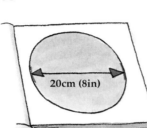

Measurements for circles show their diameter. This is how wide they are across.

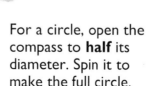

For a circle, open the compass to **half** its diameter. Spin it to make the full circle.

For a rectangle, check that the corners are square with the corner of a book.

Which glue?

The best type of glue to use is latex glue, a creamy-white glue with a 'fishy' smell. Apply a very thin layer with a spatula or brush. It works best when it begins to dry, especially if you are gluing fabric, so be patient and let it get 'tacky'. If it still doesn't work, leave it for a few more minutes.

About hems

Many fabrics fray when you cut them. This means that pieces of thread come off the edges, making them look messy. You can stop this by making a hem with glue. The instructions don't always tell you to do this, but it helps to make a neater puppet.

You don't need to hem felt, because it doesn't fray.

Put a thin layer of glue close to the edge of the fabric. Leave it to get tacky, then press the edge over.

Silly socks

You can make a funny character with just a sock, an oval of cardboard and odds and ends such as buttons, beads and scraps of fabric. Different sized ovals make different mouths, so try out smaller and bigger ones.

You will need: a sock; cardboard; glue; scraps of felt, fabric or yarn; buttons, beads (optional)

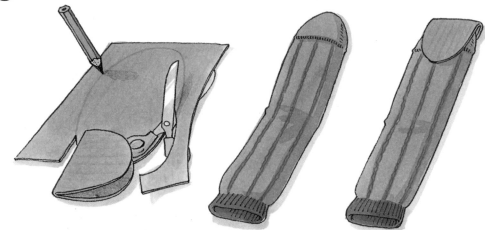

1. Cut an oval of cardboard, no wider than your sock. Fold it in half.

2. Turn the sock inside out. Flatten it so that the toe seam runs from side to side.

3. Coat the inside fold of the cardboard with glue. Press the sock into the fold as shown.

A snake is very easy to make. Use a long sock and just add a tongue and eyes.

These buttons have been sewn on, but you could glue them on.

Turn the sock so that the heel is on the top.

4. Leave the glue to dry a little, then turn the sock right side out again.

5. Pull the sock back over the cardboard until the puppet has a smiling mouth.

6. Glue on eyes and a nose. Make them from cardboard, or use an idea from the photo.

7. Add other features such as a red paper tongue, and a strip of felt or fabric for ears.

You can make a woolly wig (see steps 8-9, page 8). Trim it to make it bushy like this.

For these ears, cut two circles from another sock. Follow step 15, page 20, but don't stuff. Glue knotted ends to head. Poke hollows to make ear shape.

Finger mice

You will need:
pencil; bright paper; glue; scissors; felt-tip pens

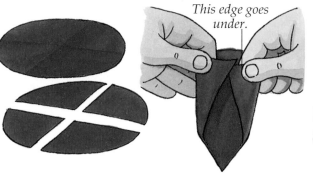

This edge goes under.

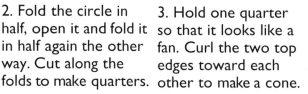

1. Draw a circle on the bright paper, about 10cm (4in) across. This is about the size of a large roll of tape, so if you have one, you could draw around it. If not, use a compass (see page 3). Cut out.

2. Fold the circle in half, open it and fold it in half again the other way. Cut along the folds to make quarters.

3. Hold one quarter so that it looks like a fan. Curl the two top edges toward each other to make a cone.

4. Hold the cone as shown. Adjust it gently until it has a point at the thin end and level edges at the wide end.

These mice are made with two circles of paper. To do this, cut two circles into quarters, then mix the quarters up.

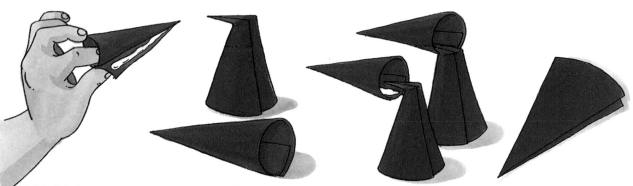

5. Hold the cone together, like this, while you put glue along the free edge. Press it into place.

6. Bend the top of the cone, bending it away from the glued edge. Make a second cone with another quarter.

7. Put glue inside the second cone, where the paper overlaps. Press the flap of the first cone over it.

8. Fold a third quarter in half. Draw an ear shape. Make the folded edge one edge of the ear, as shown.

Trim the ears to a smaller shape if you want to.

Round the paws with scissors.

9. Cut out the ear shape. It will open out into a heart shape. Fold the tip of the shape, as shown.

10. Put glue on the tip of the ear shape. Stick it into the top of the head cone, directly above the body cone.

11. Fold the last quarter in half. Cut a strip 7mm (¼in) wide down the longest open edge. These are the 'arms'.

12. Open out the arms and glue them to the back of the mouse with the paws pointing up.

Fold

13. For the eyes, draw a shape on what's left of your paper, as shown here. Cut it out, then open it out.

14. Fold the straight edge under. Add pupils with a felt-tip pen if you want. Glue to the mouse's head.

7

Glove puppets

For each puppet you will need:
two large sheets of newspaper; leg of a pair of tights; thin cardboard (in different shades if you want); ball of yarn; container such as bottle; bright felt or fabric; masking tape; felt-tip pens; tracing paper; cork or other 'nose'; other decorations (optional)

Making a head

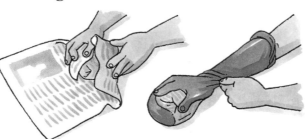

It helps to hold this arm next to your body.

1. Crumple one sheet of newspaper into a ball, then wrap the other sheet around it to make the ball's surface smoother.

2. Push the ball into the tights' leg, right down to the end. Keep your hand inside the tights and pull the tights up to your elbow.

3. Twist the ball around once with your other hand. Pull the tights down over your hand and all the way over the ball.

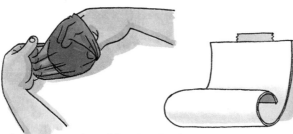

Tie the loose ends around the neck.

4. Put your hand back into tights. As before, twist the ball and pull the tights over. Repeat until the tights are used up.

5. Cut a piece of cardboard 15 x 10cm (6 x 4in). Roll it into a tube big enough for a finger to fit into. Tape it with masking tape.

6. Use scissors to snip a hole in the bottom of the head. Make it bigger with your fingers. Put some glue into it, then push the tube in.

7. Make a mouth and eyes out of cardboard (see photo for ideas). Glue them onto the puppet head. Glue the cork 'nose' into place.

For hair like this, coat head with glue. Wrap yarn around it. Glue on another little ball for a bun.

Glue lace around neck and wrists.

8. For hair, wrap yarn around the container. (For long hair, use a big container). Tie the strands together with an extra strand.

9. Snip the strands opposite the knot, on the other side of the container. Put glue over the head and stick the 'wig' on.

Making the glove body

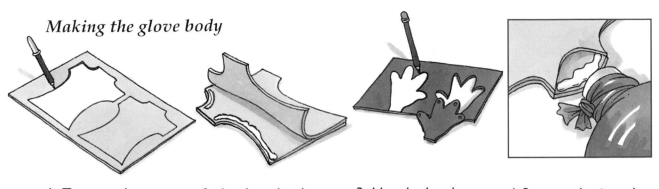

1. Trace and cut out the glove body template on page 30. Draw around it twice on the fabric or felt. Cut the shapes out.

2. Apply a thin layer of glue to the wrong side of one piece, as shown. Press the other piece on top of it, wrong side down.

3. Use the hand template on page 30 to cut out two hands in cardboard. Decorate them with felt-tip pens if you want.

4. Squeeze glue into the sleeves and neck gap. Put the hands into the sleeves. Press firmly. Position the head in the neck gap.

How to hold your puppet

To bring your puppet to life, hold it as shown here, with your first finger inside the tube.

Make a smaller nose by cutting a cork in half.

You can cut felt shapes and glue them on.

Fruity milkshakes

These are rod puppets. They have two rods, one to hold them by, and another to make them look as though they're talking and making funny faces.

For each milkshake, you will need: thin cardboard; large roll adhesive tape; craft knife; about 30 x 23cm (12 x 9in) felt (a fruity shade); glue; two thin sticks 30cm (12in) long; felt-tip pens or crayons; sheet of newspaper; cotton balls; two drinking straws

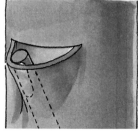

The square should be opposite the stick.

1. Cut cardboard, 60 x 23cm (24 x 9in). Roll it up. Put inside roll of tape. Let it spring out. Tape as shown. Remove roll of tape. Tape a stick over the top.

2. Draw a square, 5 x 5cm (2 x 2in), 10cm (4in) down the tube. Make a slit with the craft knife, then cut the square out. Cut through all the layers.

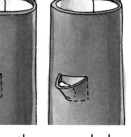

3. Cut enough felt to cover the tube. Put glue along one edge. Press the tube to it. Glue the other edge. Roll the tube around and press it down.

4. Feel for the square hole through the felt and cut a slit along the top edge. Put a dab of glue in the middle of the bottom 'lip', on the inside.

5. Poke the other stick up through the tube until level with the bottom lip. Press to the glue, then let it dry **for at least twenty minutes.**

You don't need to pull the mouth rod very hard.

6. While the mouth glue is drying, make the eyes out of cardboard, and fruit shapes to match the felt (see the photograph for more ideas).

7. Put glue around the inside rim at the top. Crumple a sheet of newspaper. Place it in the top. Cover with cotton balls. Glue on straws, fruit and eyes.

8. To work the puppet, hold the back rod in one hand. Make it talk by moving the mouth rod around with your other hand.

Chatty carrot

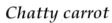

You need: same as for milkshakes (but no newspaper, cotton balls or straws); tissue paper and pipe cleaners; needle and thread. Use a bigger piece of felt.

1. Follow steps 1-2 (left), but make tube 18 x 60cm (7 x 24in). Cut felt 20cm (8in) longer than tube.

2. Place tube on felt leaving 15cm (6in) at the bottom and 5cm (2in) at the top. Draw a 'roof' shape, as shown. Cut along these lines.

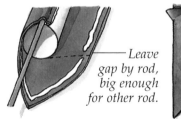

Leave gap by rod, big enough for other rod.

3. Glue along sides, down to the point. Press rod to one edge, then roll tube to meet other edge. Press bottom into a point, then follow steps 4-5.

4. Sew around top edge, pull ends tight and knot. Glue pieces of tissue paper to pipe cleaners. Glue into top of carrot. Make eyes. Glue on.

Greedy hamburgers

These puppets are mouth puppets. The moving part is a big mouth which you can open wide and snap shut again.

You will need: 33 x 18cm (13 x 7in) dark brown felt; 50 x 25cm (20 x 10in) light brown felt; thin cardboard; stuffing such as cotton balls or newspaper; a large clip; red felt; yellow felt; green tissue paper; felt-tip pens

You need two circle shapes to draw around, one 16cm (6in) across, the other 24cm (9½in). Make templates (see page 3), or use lids or plates of about the right size.

You can glue grains of rice to the top of the burger to look like sesame seeds, or little glass beads to look like poppy seeds.

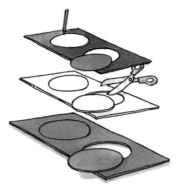

1. Draw the smaller circle shape twice on dark brown felt, then on cardboard. Draw the larger shape twice on light brown felt. Cut them all out.

2. Put a layer of glue around the edge of one dark brown circle, leaving a gap as shown. Press the other circle on top of it and leave to dry.

3. Glue around the edge of a cardboard circle, leaving a gap. Place on a light felt circle. Turn edges over by pressing down, pinching, then pressing again.

Gap

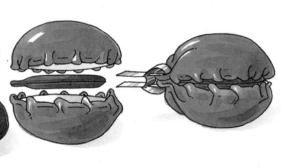

4. Repeat with the other two circles. Allow to dry for five minutes, then stuff both 'bun' shapes until rounded and firm. Glue edges over at the gaps.

5. Gently turn the dark brown circles inside out. This is the 'burger'. Put glue just inside and around the edges of the opening.

6. Place the burger between the buns so that all three are glued together at one edge. Use a large clip to hold them together until the glue dries.

'Lettuce' 'Cheese'

'Ketchup' 'Onions'

Make sure the 'ketchup' has a tongue.

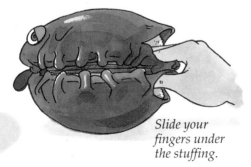

Slide your fingers under the stuffing.

7. Roughly cut an oval of tissue paper, a square of yellow felt and a blob of red felt. Cut a circle of white cardboard, then cut it into a spiral.

8. Make round cardboard eyes. Glue the lettuce under the burger. Glue the cheese, onions and ketchup on top of the burger. Glue on the eyes.

9. At the back of the burger, snip a 7cm (3in) slit in the top bun and a 3cm (1in) slit in the bottom bun, where shown. Slide your hand into the slits.

13

Rock singer

Like the milkshakes, this puppet is a rod puppet. It has flexible arms that you can move into different positions.

You will need: thin cardboard; 30 x 90cm (12 x 36in) felt (this can be in three pieces); stick 60cm (24in) long; small piece other felt; ball of yarn; felt-tip pens; plastic bottle about 30cm (12in) high; 60 x 60cm (24 x 24in) fabric; craft knife; stuffing (cotton balls); 75cm (2½ft) stiff wire; kitchen foil; tape

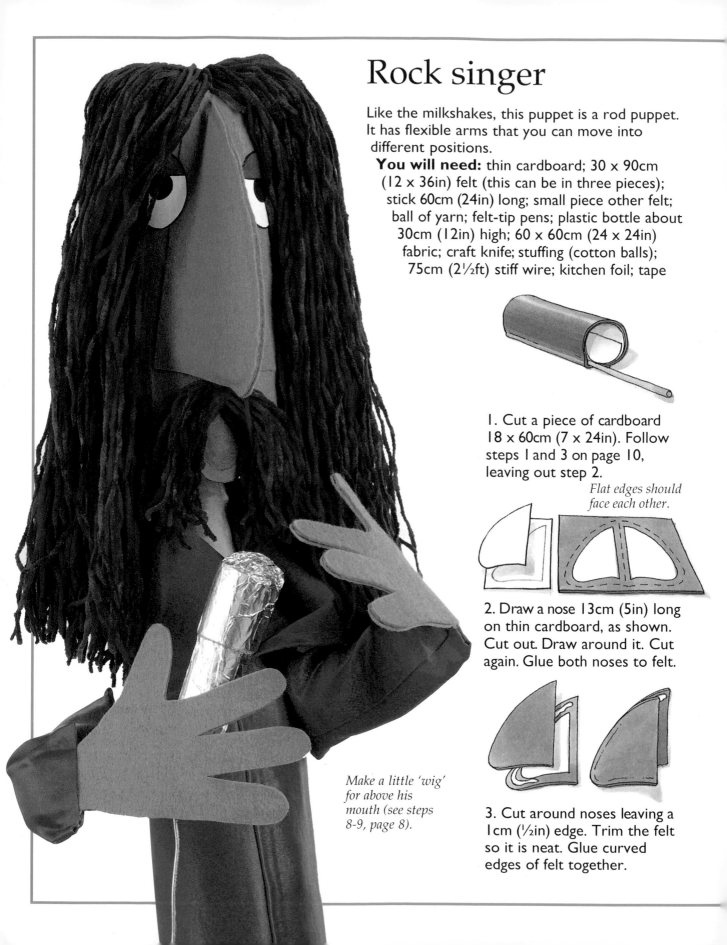

1. Cut a piece of cardboard 18 x 60cm (7 x 24in). Follow steps 1 and 3 on page 10, leaving out step 2.

Flat edges should face each other.

2. Draw a nose 13cm (5in) long on thin cardboard, as shown. Cut out. Draw around it. Cut again. Glue both noses to felt.

Make a little 'wig' for above his mouth (see steps 8-9, page 8).

3. Cut around noses leaving a 1cm (½in) edge. Trim the felt so it is neat. Glue curved edges of felt together.

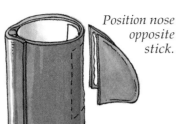
Position nose opposite stick.

Arrange hair so it covers top of tube.

4. Open out straight edges of nose slightly. Put glue along them and position them carefully on the face. Press.

5. Make hair (see steps 8-9, page 8.) Put glue around top of head. Arrange hair over it. Make eyes and mouth. Glue on.

6. Cut a piece of the second felt, 10 x 15cm (4 x 6in). Glue it around the top of the bottle to make a shirt.

Make hems if your fabric frays.

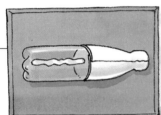

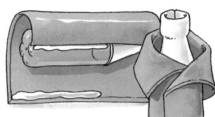

7. Cut fabric to cover bottle, allowing an extra 5cm (2in) at top and bottom. Put a strip of glue along the bottle.

8. Place glued strip on edge of fabric. Glue other edge, but not the neck area. Roll bottle onto it. Fold 'collar' back.

9. For sleeves, cut fabric 13 x 13cm (5 x 5in), twice. Glue one edge of each sleeve. Fold and press down as shown.

Use template on page 30 for hands.

Don't glue wire to fabric.

10. Cut two cardboard hands. Glue to felt. Cut out. Turn over and repeat. Glue one side of hands into sleeves.

11. With a craft knife, carefully cut slits through the fabric and the bottle at the 'shoulder' on both sides.

12. Stuff the arms. Push the wire up one sleeve, through slits and down other sleeve. Glue sleeves shut at shoulder.

Make end of microphone bigger with more foil.

Cut slit here.

Tape

13. Glue end of the wire to one wrist. Glue sleeve over it. Pull wire gently at other end so that arms touch shoulders.

14. Glue wire into other sleeve. Bend down as shown. For microphone, make cardboard tube. Wrap in foil. Glue on.

15. Cut a slit in bottom of the bottle. Push head rod through, then wrap tape around rod to stop bottle from slipping off.

Shadow puppets

Shadow puppets show up on a screen when a light is shone on them from behind. The ones shown here are based on templates on page 32, but you can draw any shape you like.

You will need:
cardboard; drinking straws that bend at the end; tape; paper fasteners; string or feathers (optional)

A shadow fish

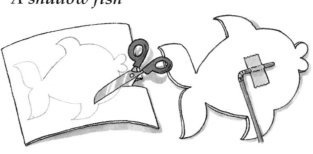

1. Draw a fish on thin cardboard (see template on page 32). Cut it out.

2. Bend a straw and trim the bent end to leave about 3cm (1in). Tape it to the fish.

3. You could add pieces of string to make the tail wavy, or a feather for a fin.

A snapping shark

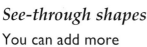

1. Draw a shark's body on thin cardboard (use template on page 32). Cut it out. Make a hole where shown.

2. Draw the jaw on thin cardboard using the jaw template. Cut it out. Make a hole where shown.

3. Position the two holes over each other. Push a paper fastener through them. Open it out at the back.

4. Tape a bent straw to the body and another to the jaw. Use both hands to make the shark snap.

See-through shapes

You can add more detail to your puppets and make them brighter by creating a see-through effect with cooking oil.

You will need:
the same as above, but also: bright felt-tip pens; paper towels; cooking oil; newspaper

Use templates on page 32.

1. Cut shapes out of cardboard, as above. Place on newspaper. Decorate on one side with felt-tip pens.

2. Use a paper towel to dab oil over both sides of the shapes. Let oil soak in, then wipe shapes dry.

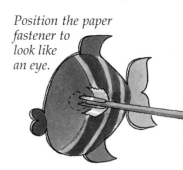

Position the paper fastener to look like an eye.

3. Push a paper fastener through the puppet, but don't bend it back. Tape it to a straight straw.

Making a shadow puppet screen

You will need: a large cardboard box; large sheet of tracing paper; desk lamp; tape

1. Cut out the bottom of the box, leaving 2cm (1in) all the way around. Cut the tracing paper to fit neatly inside the box.

2. Tape the tracing paper inside the hole. Make scenery in the same way as the see-through puppets, but without the controls.

3. Glue the scenery onto the tracing paper inside the box. Place the lamp behind the box so that it shines onto the screen.

When you have made the screen, stand behind the light and lean over it, holding the puppets in front of it. Press them firmly against the screen and move them around. For the best effect, give your show in a dark room so that your audience just sees the puppets.

Clown puppet

This puppet takes a while to make as there are lots of steps, but each step is fairly easy. It is well worth the effort, because this is a very expressive puppet who can make different faces and use his arms too.

How to hold the clown

One hand goes up through the kilt and shirt and into the head and chin. The other hand holds the wires.

You can sew or glue small buttons to the front of the shirt.

You will need: thin white cardboard; stiff cardboard; newspaper; two 40cm (16in) strips of ribbon; four bright buttons; felt-tip pens; pencil; 90cm (3ft) strong wire; two paper clips; strong thread; large needle; glue; scissors; craft knife; skewer

You will also need: 'skin' felt 60 x 50cm (24 x 20in); red felt 30 x 30cm (12 x 12in); blue felt for mouth and hands 45 x 30cm (18 x 12in); scraps of blue and black felt for eyelids and pupils; other fabrics — see shirt, kilt and hair below

Make templates for the shapes below (see page 3). Be careful not to mix them up once you have cut them.

When you glue felt to felt, you must let the glue get tacky (see page 3). The instructions remind you by saying 'leave'.

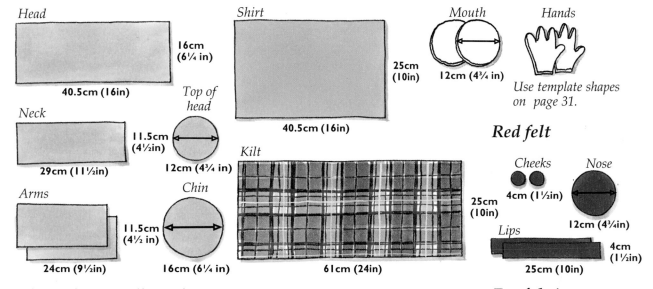

'Skin' felt

Head
16cm (6¼ in)
40.5cm (16in)

Neck
29cm (11½in)

Arms
11.5cm (4½ in)
24cm (9½in)

Top of head
11.5cm (4½in)
12cm (4¾ in)

Chin
11.5cm (4½ in)
16cm (6¼ in)

Bright fabrics or felt

Shirt
25cm (10in)
40.5cm (16in)

Kilt
61cm (24in)

Stiff cardboard

Mouth
12cm (4¾ in)

Hands
Use template shapes on page 31.

Red felt

Cheeks
4cm (1½in)

Nose
12cm (4¾in)

25cm (10in)

Lips
25cm (10in)
4cm (1½in)

Thin white cardboard

Waistband
61cm (24 in)
2.5cm (1in)

Eyes and ears
Use template shapes on page 31.

Fur fabric

Hair
8cm (3in)
25cm (10in)

How to make the clown

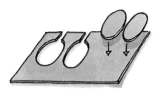   

1. Glue one side of cardboard ear pieces to 'skin' felt. Cut out. Glue the other side and repeat.

2. Glue one side of the hands onto the blue felt. Cut them out. Glue the other side and repeat.

3. Coat one side of cardboard mouth circles with glue. Press onto same felt as hands. Cut out.

4. Glue along narrow edges of head and neck felt. Press edges down. When dry, turn inside out.

The clown continues on the next page

The clown (continued)

Leave a 8cm (3in) gap in the glue on the chin and one mouth.

Match the gaps together.

Don't pull the felt too tight.

The felt won't need 'pinching' very much.

5. Glue around the edge of the 'chin' felt, the felt side of the mouth circles and one edge of the head, on the inside. Leave.

6. Put the mouth with the gap on the chin felt, sticky side up. Turn the edges using the 'pinch and press' method (see step 3, page 13).

7. Fit the other mouth circle just inside the head, felt side up. 'Pinch and press' the edges of the head over onto the glue.

8. Turn the head over and sew around the other edge, about 1cm (½in) from the top. Use big stitches. Leave long threads.

Leave 2½ cm (1in) empty at the top.

Trim threads after knotting.

9. Scrunch sheets of newspaper in from the edge to make 'pads', smooth on one side. Fit them into the head, crumpled side down.

10. Pull the threads tight on the top of the head and knot. Put glue on the top of the head circle. Position it over the head.

11. Stuff the 'chin' with scraps of newspaper. Put some glue where you left a gap on the chin piece. Leave to get tacky.

12. Place the head on top of the chin and press to the glue. Snip a 8cm (3in) slit in the head, about 1cm (½in) from the bottom.

Knot the threads as tightly as you can.

13. Draw a circle 9cm (3½in) across with a felt-tip pen as shown. Glue around one edge of the neck, on the inside. Leave.

14. Using the circle you have drawn as a guide, carefully position the neck over the head and chin. Press it into place.

15. For the nose, sew around the edge using big stitches. Put a small ball of newspaper in the middle. Draw threads tight, knot and trim.

16. On the eyes, coat the eyelid area with glue. Cover with felt and trim to shape. Add black felt circles for pupils.

17. Glue back of nose and eyes, and one side of cheeks and lips. Leave, then press onto face. The lips fit around mouth as shown.

18. Put a line of glue down one side of each ear. Position above end of lips as shown. Allow to dry. When dry, fold back.

19. Glue short ends of hair under to make hems. Position hair around head to see where ears are. Make slits for ears. Glue on.

20. Glue along one side of each arm. Fold the other edge over and press down. Glue inside one end of both arms. Press hands in.

Glue the shorter edge.

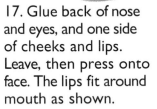
   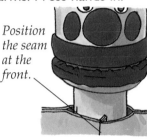

Position the seam at the front.

21. Glue one edge of body piece, on the right side. Fold other edge onto it. When dry enough, turn inside out. Repeat with kilt.

22. Glue waistband ends together. Fit inside kilt, with 1cm (½in) fabric showing at top. Glue, then turn fabric over.

23. Glue a button to the ends of both strips of ribbon. Glue the ribbons to the top of the kilt, crossing them over each other.

24. Put 2cm (¾in) band of glue around the inside of the body, at the top. Place the neck in the middle and press the edges down.

 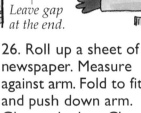 *Leave gap at the end.*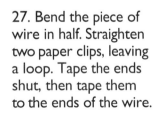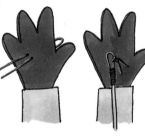

25. Put the body into the kilt, making sure the straps cross at the back. Glue the straps into position behind the shoulders.

26. Roll up a sheet of newspaper. Measure against arm. Fold to fit and push down arm. Glue ends shut. Glue arms to back of puppet.

27. Bend the piece of wire in half. Straighten two paper clips, leaving a loop. Tape the ends shut, then tape them to the ends of the wire.

28. Poke two holes very carefully in each hand with a skewer. Sew through holes with thread. Knot the paper clips to each hand.

21

King on strings

This puppet is a marionette, or string puppet.

You will need: large yogurt carton; felt for skin; red felt; thin cardboard; felt-tip pens; newspaper; paints; plastic bottle about 25cm (10in) high; 60 x 60cm (24 x 24in) fabric for body and sleeves; craft knife; 70 x 70cm (28 x 28in) fabric for cloak; 50cm (20in) string; doily; needle; 60cm (24in) braid; pencil; strong thread; two paper clips; tape

Measure carton to judge length of nose.

1. Cover yogurt carton with 'skin' felt (see step 3, page 10). Cut a little extra to glue under bottom edge. Draw around carton on felt. Cut out.

2. Glue circle of felt to bottom of carton. Make nose (see steps 2-3, page 14, but smaller to fit carton) and cardboard eyes. Glue on.

Paint the crown with yellow or gold paint.

The circle needs to be about 25cm (10in) across.

If bottle is round, you don't need to pad it.

Fold under

3. Make ears (see step 1, page 19). Glue on. Cut strip of cardboard to fit around head. Cut into crown shape, then glue edges together.

4. In the same way as the nose on page 20, (step 15) make 'pad' of red felt to fit inside the crown. Glue into crown. Glue crown to head.

5. Tape a pad of newspaper to the plastic bottle. Cut enough fabric to cover body. Wrap around body and glue in place, but don't glue the neck yet.

Make the join in the middle.

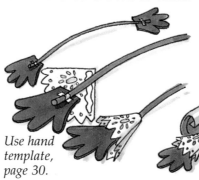

Use hand template, page 30.

Fold this edge under.

You can hem the ends of the sleeves to make them neater.

6. With a craft knife, carefully cut a flap in the bottom of the head. Fold back and wedge the bottle neck into it. Arrange and glue fabric around neck.

7. Cut two cardboard hands. Cover in felt (see step 2, page 19). Tape the string to each wrist. Glue on cones made of doily pieces to hide the tape.

8. Cut fabric 18 x 45cm (7 x 18in). Place hands and rope along the middle of it. Fold the fabric and glue, as shown. Glue to back of puppet.

9. Cut cloak fabric same height as king and three times as wide. Hem edges. At the top, make a big hem (to half the height of head).

10. Glue braid on right side of fabric, just below the level of the top hem. Tie around king's neck.

Making the controls

Tape a paper clip to each end of the pencil so that a loop sticks out. Cut 122cm (4ft) strong thread and thread needle.

Sew through one wrist. Knot. Thread needle again, take through one paper clip and sew through other wrist. Knot.

Cut thread 90cm (3ft) long. Repeat as above, but this time knot the thread to the ears and pass it through the other paper clip.

Glue on a brooch and pieces of doily at the neck.

A shining knight

You will need: newspaper; white tights; cotton balls; clear tape; scissors; kitchen foil; 90cm (3ft) stiff wire; pliers; strong thread; large needle; felt-tip pens; pencil; ruler; three corks; plastic bottle about 15cm (6in) high; skewer; thin cardboard; thick cardboard

Out of thin cardboard, cut:
Four rectangles 15 x 8cm (6 x 3in) for arms
Four rectangles 15 x 10cm (6 x 4in) for legs
One rectangle 35 x 15cm (14 x 6in) for helmet
A shield and a sword (see templates, page 31)
Two hands (see template page 31)
Out of thick cardboard, cut: one rectangle 10 x 4cm (4 x 1½in) for control bar

Use fur fabric if you have some.

1. Make a head with newspaper and tights (see steps 1-4, page 6). Knot loose ends at the neck. Make eyes. Glue them on.

2. For a nose, stuff a scrap of tights with a cotton ball. Knot. Glue on. Glue on tufts of cotton balls for other features.

 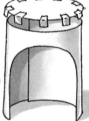 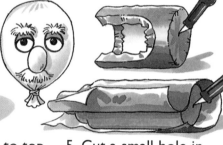 

3. Measure helmet rectangle around head and tape to fit. Take off. Draw a circle around it on thin cardboard. Cut it out.

4. Tape circle to top of helmet. Draw shape to fit around face, as shown. It helps to measure the width of the face first. Cut out.

5. Cut a small hole in top of helmet and bottom of bottle. Coat both in glue and wrap in foil. Cut foil and glue edges over to fit.

6. Glue foil over hands, sword, shield and two corks. For flat pieces, it helps to cover one side, cut it out, then cover other side.

Legs are two long tubes, arms two short tubes.

 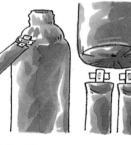

7. Tape arm and leg rectangles into tubes about 2cm (¾in) wide. Glue foil over them, tucking it in at the ends. Press ends flat.

8. Make joints with clear tape. Make a flap of clear tape at the top of each arm and leg by folding it over as shown.

9. Tape hands to arms. Make sure the thumbs point up. Tape corks to legs, making sure the flattened part of the legs face forward.

10. Tape the arm flaps to each 'shoulder' of the bottle. Tape the leg flaps to the back of the bottle, at the bottom.

24

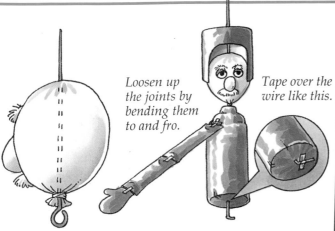

Loosen up the joints by bending them to and fro.

Tape over the wire like this.

11. Make a hole in the head very carefully with a skewer. Poke up from the knot and come out at the top of the head.

12. Push the wire through helmet, head and bottle. Use pliers to bend it at right angles at the bottom. Tape it into position.

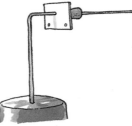

13. Carefully make holes with a skewer in the control bar and cork, where shown. Glue the cork over the middle hole.

14. Bend the wire back at right angles 30cm (1ft) above the helmet. Slide the cork and control bar onto the wire.

Tape the shield and sword to the knight's hands.

The knight shows up well against a bright background like this.

15. Bend wire up and around so that it points as shown. Tape paper clip to the end, leaving a loop free for threading through.

See next page for how to string this puppet.

A string puppet show

You will need: four chairs you can tie sticks to; four long sticks such as garden canes; two big pieces of fabric; masking tape; string; cardboard and paints for scenery (optional)

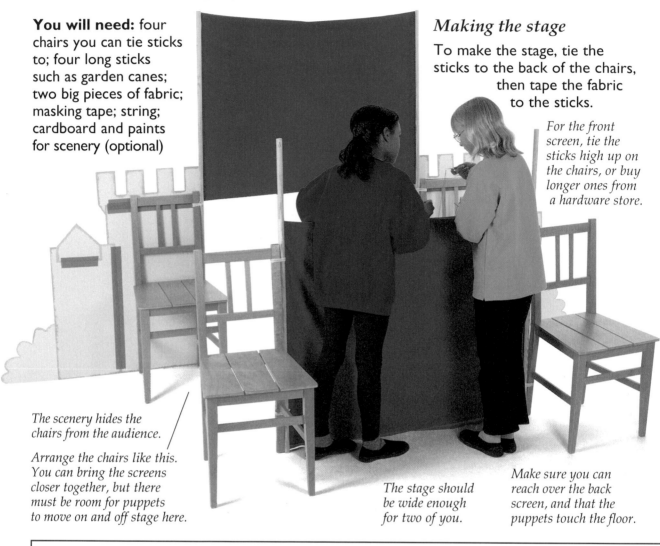

The scenery hides the chairs from the audience.

Arrange the chairs like this. You can bring the screens closer together, but there must be room for puppets to move on and off stage here.

Making the stage

To make the stage, tie the sticks to the back of the chairs, then tape the fabric to the sticks.

For the front screen, tie the sticks high up on the chairs, or buy longer ones from a hardware store.

The stage should be wide enough for two of you.

Make sure you can reach over the back screen, and that the puppets touch the floor.

How to string the knight

You need to hold the puppet firmly to string it properly. The trickiest part is getting the leg threads the right length. The key to this is holding the control bar at right angles to the wire, and the puppet's knee straight. It helps a lot if you have a friend who can hold it while you pull the thread.

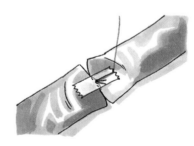

1. Cut two pieces of thread about 90cm (3ft) long. Tie each one around a knee joint and secure with clear tape.

Ask your friend to hold the knee straight.

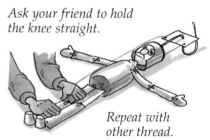

Repeat with other thread.

2. Holding bar at right angles to wire, push thread through its hole. With knee straight, pull the thread tight. Knot.

This is how the show looks from the front. Your audience will get the best view if they sit on the floor.

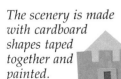

Try shining a light onto the stage to create a spotlight effect.

The scenery is made with cardboard shapes taped together and painted.

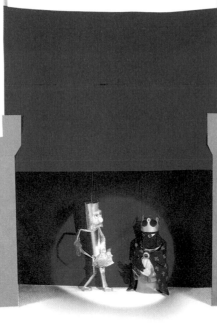

Tips for putting on a show

The puppet should look as though it is standing naturally.

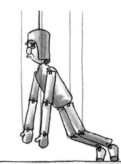

Lifting a puppet up spoils the impression that it is moving by itself.

Make sure your puppets touch the ground, or they will look as though they are flying.

They shouldn't 'sink' into the stage and look as though they are dragging themselves along.

Bring puppets on from the left or right, not from above, unless you want them to 'fly'.

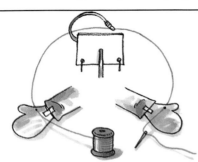

3. Thread needle, but don't cut thread. Sew through one wrist, up through paper clip and down to other wrist.

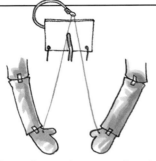

4. Sew through second wrist and knot. At first wrist, pull thread so that arms are bent slightly. Cut and knot thread.

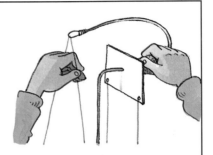

5. To make the knight walk, hold the cork and rock it to and fro. Move his arms by pulling the arm strings.

Glove and rod puppet shows

For puppets that you hold up, such as glove or rod puppets, you need to make just one screen that hides you completely. Make it in the same way as the back screen on pages 26-27.

You will need: two chairs that you can tie sticks to; two long sticks; large piece of fabric such as an old sheet (dark fabric is best because it hides you better than light fabric); masking tape; string; cardboard and paints for scenery (optional)

The chairs make a good place to keep the puppets when you are not using them.

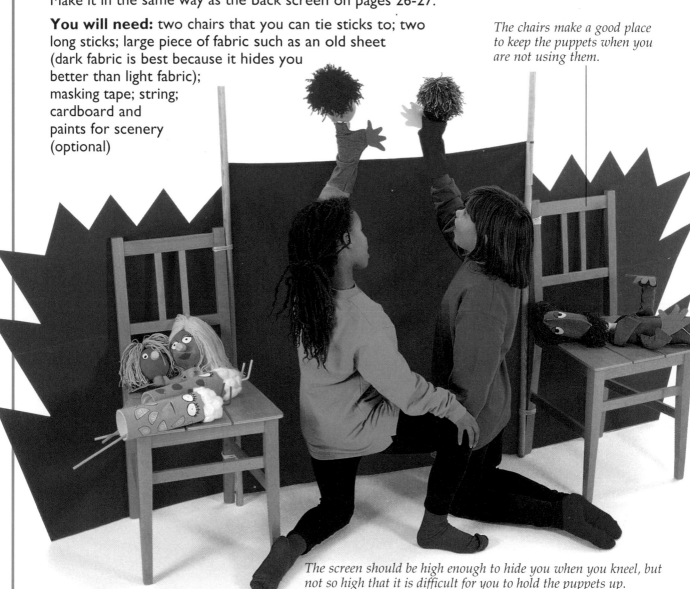

The screen should be high enough to hide you when you kneel, but not so high that it is difficult for you to hold the puppets up.

Telling a story

1. Keep your stories short and simple. If your story is long and complicated, you may forget parts of it, and your arms will get very tired.

2. Make the puppets talk one at a time. Move the puppet that is talking in time to your voice. Keep the other puppets still.

3. Use voices that you know you can keep on doing. Speak clearly, so that the audience can hear easily, and don't talk too fast.

Holding the puppets

This puppet is sinking out of view.

Move your puppet as though it is walking off the stage.

1. Puppets should look out at the audience, unless they are talking to each other. Then the puppet which is talking should face the other one.

2. Try not to let your puppets 'sink' as your arm gets tired. The audience should see most of their bodies as well as their heads.

3. When your puppets are leaving the stage, take them off at the sides. It looks very strange if they suddenly drop down out of view.

Performing without a stage

Some puppets, such as the clown, work well without a stage. You can sit holding it on a chair or stool in front of your audience, then talk to it and make it talk back.

Try to make your puppet look as though it is moving on its own. Speak to it as if it can really hear you. Move it so that it looks around and makes funny faces.

When you pretend that it is speaking, use a different voice and try to make its mouth move in time to what it says. Move its arms around to give it extra expression.

29

Templates

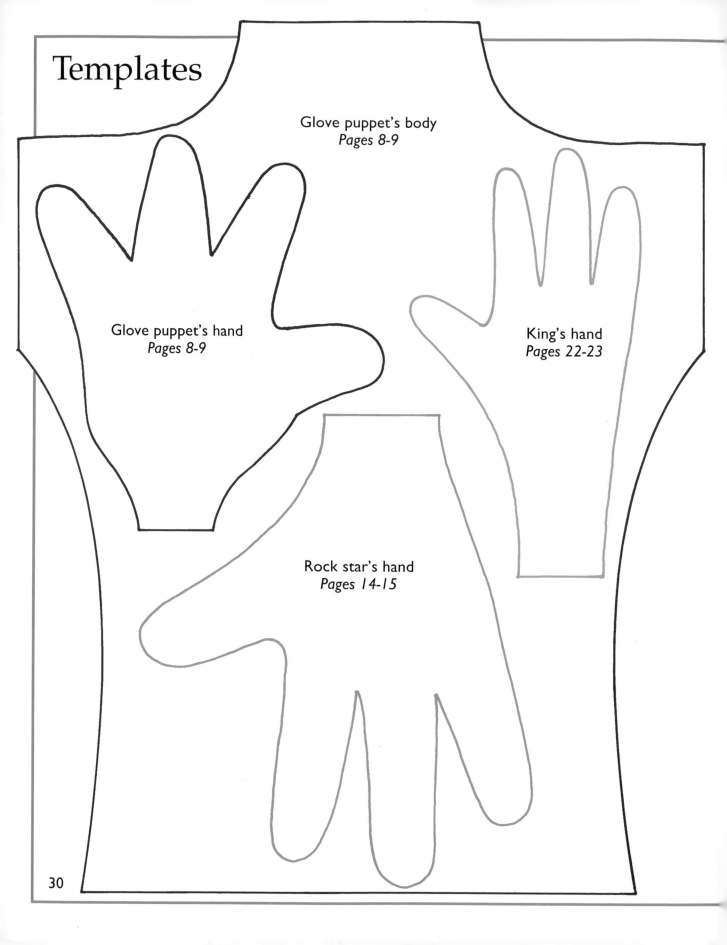

Glove puppet's body
Pages 8-9

Glove puppet's hand
Pages 8-9

King's hand
Pages 22-23

Rock star's hand
Pages 14-15

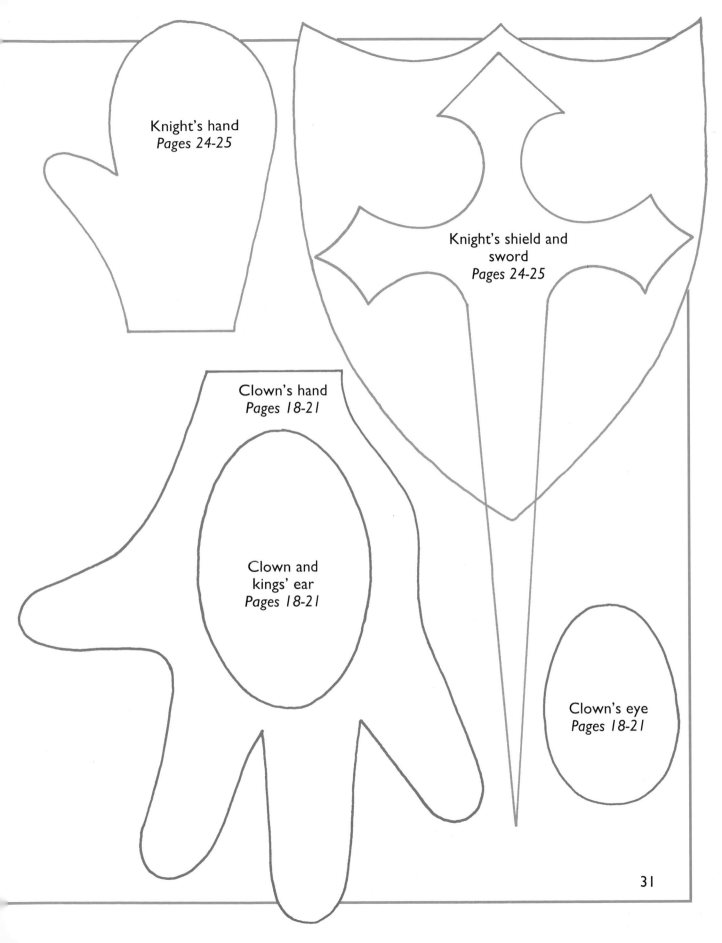

Knight's hand
Pages 24-25

Knight's shield and
sword
Pages 24-25

Clown's hand
Pages 18-21

Clown and
kings' ear
Pages 18-21

Clown's eye
Pages 18-21

31

Templates

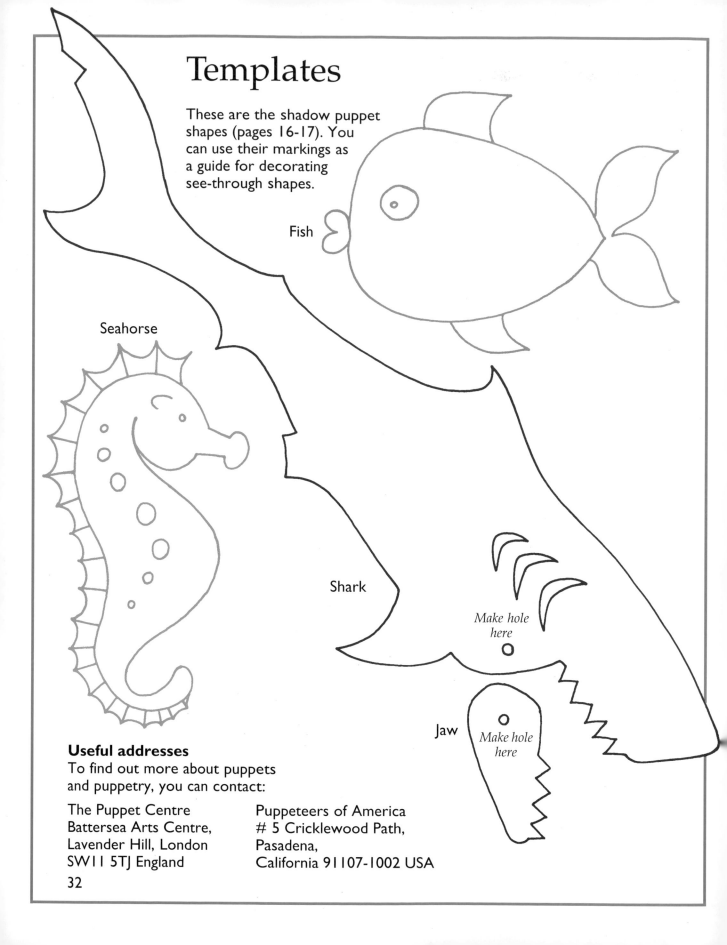

These are the shadow puppet shapes (pages 16-17). You can use their markings as a guide for decorating see-through shapes.

Fish

Seahorse

Shark

Make hole here

Jaw

Make hole here

Useful addresses

To find out more about puppets and puppetry, you can contact:

The Puppet Centre
Battersea Arts Centre,
Lavender Hill, London
SW11 5TJ England

Puppeteers of America
5 Cricklewood Path,
Pasadena,
California 91107-1002 USA